THE
LOSER
LIST
JINX OF THE LOSER

Also by H.N. Kowitt

THE LOSER LIST

LIST

JINX OF THE LOSER

Written and Illustrated by

H.N. KOWITT

SCHOLASTIC PRESS / NEW YORK

ISBN 978-0-545-50794-3

Text copyright © 2013 by Holly Kowitt

Illustrations copyright © 2013 by Scholastic Inc.

All rights reserved. Published by Scholastic Press,

an imprint of Scholastic Inc., Publishers since 1920.

SCHOLASTIC, SCHOLASTIC PRESS, and associated logos are

trademarks and/or registered trademarks of Scholastic Inc.

12 11 10 9 8 7 6 5 4 3 2 1   13 14 15 16 17 18/0

Printed in the U.S.A.   23

First printing, May 2013

For Stephanie Stone and Lisa Leventer

Special thanks to David Manis and
Ellen Miles

* ME AT-A-GLANCE

Name: Danny Shine (rhymes with "whine")

Age: 12

School: Gerald Ford Middle School

Often found at: Comix Nation

Never found at: Cafeteria "cool" table

Secret weapon: Drawing rude tattoos

Likes: Pizza Day, Asia O'Neill

Hates: Gym, Swirlies, Mexican wedgies

Least likely to: Shave a Chicago Bears logo into my head

Burning question: "Does this zombie need more drool?"

* CHAPTER ONE *

I began the day as Danny Shine, invisible seventh-grade comic book geek. When it ended, I was the Guy Who'd Destroyed Everyone's Hopes and Dreams. I was booed, jeered at, even spit on — kids hated me so much, I needed a security guard just to walk down the street.

It started at the All-City Baseball Championships.

My best friend, Jasper, and I were in the front row at Hartman Field, a baseball stadium across town, watching beefy jocks high-five each other. For the first time in twenty-five years, Gerald Ford Middle School had a shot at clinching the city baseball title. GF had never seen a winning season, much less a _championship._

All week, the whole school was breathless, asking, "Is the 'Curse of the Woodchucks' finally over?"

Jasper and I couldn't care less.

"Why are we here again?" Jasper asked.

"Asia O'Neill gave me tickets." I wanted to keep explanations short. My crush on her was so secret, even Jasper didn't know about it. "She couldn't use them."

"Why didn't you just say we were busy?" Jasper asked, turning the page of his comic book. To get him to come, I'd had to bribe him with a rare first edition of Rat Girl. I didn't think he'd read it during the game.

"I just thought it would be a goof." The truth was too embarrassing. A few days ago, Asia had come up to me at lunch.

"Hey, Danny," she'd said. "Want to go to All-City on Sunday?"

The coolest girl I knew was asking me to do something! This was so off the charts, I didn't know how to process it.

"Y-yeah. Sure. Absolutely."

"Oh, good." She sounded relieved. "See, Jenna and I are going rock climbing Saturday and can't use our tickets."

WHAT?

CRUD! I felt like I'd just been punched.

"I didn't even know if you liked baseball," she said.

"Uh . . ." I didn't want her to think I'd said yes only because I thought she was going. "Yeah. Totally. Big fan."

"Good."

"Can't wait to see those stupid . . . other guys get pounded," I added.

"Highland, you mean," she said.

"Right."

Just remembering that conversation made me cringe. Now Jasper and I were sitting behind third base, surrounded by a sea of Woodchuck fans wearing orange and blue. Across the field, maroon and silver flags waved for the Silver Hawks, the defending champs from snooty Highland Middle School. The stadium was a neutral site, but both schools had tons of fans there.

"All this hoopla," I said, turning to Jasper. "what's the point? It's just a bunch of overgrown freaks hitting a ball around." In my opinion, the wrong things in life got all the attention:

Sports

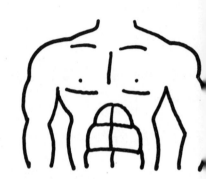

Ripped abs

Good looks

"Right now we could be having a James Bond marathon," Jasper pointed out. On Saturdays, we sometimes watched back-to-back movies or hung at our favorite store, Comix Nation. "How long does this go on for?"

"It's only the first inning," I said.

"So, what, two more to go?"

"More like eight." I don't know that much about sports, but next to Jasper? I might as well be the commissioner of baseball.

"In that case..." Jasper opened up his bag to show a stack of comics. "Want some reading material?"

Jasper didn't care what people thought, which I admired. He just did his own weird thing, whether it was turtle racing, designing robots, or whatever. But I was too self-conscious to sit in the bleachers and read, so I shook my head.

"I guess we could stay until halftime," Jasper said.

"Baseball doesn't have —"

I didn't get to finish. Someone elbowed me to stand, and suddenly we were swept up in "the wave."

Behind us were a bunch of obnoxious, face-painted jocks from school. There was Tank Friedman, a football player whose head was shaped like a canned ham. Next to him were his friends Kyle Larson and "Abs" Tanaka.

"HIGHLAND REEKS!" Tank yelled, his face half blue, half orange. Tank represented everything I didn't like about jocks. Rude, loud, and cocky, he acted like he owned the school. He and Kyle were throwing French fries at each other.

I tried to focus on the field. A Silver Hawk batter came to the plate. "That's Dex Van Zandt," someone behind me said. "He's their best hitter."

"STRIKE 'EM OUT!" our cheerleaders yelled. I spotted an enormous coil of hair with orange and blue feathers in it and recognized Chantal Davis, the bossiest diva in seventh grade. The cheering squad leaped around while Chantal browbeat the fans by megaphone.

"Are you people _dead_?" she yelled. "I can't hear you!"

"Woodchucks are number one!" the crowd chanted.

"_People_." Chantal shook her head. "Show these Highland clowns we got the skills to pay the bills. You feel me?"

"WOODCHUCKS ARE NUMBER ONE!"

"Got _that_ right," Chantal said. Being a cheerleader was the perfect job for her. She got to bully people on a mass scale.

As if to prove Chantal wrong, Dex hit a long line drive into deep left field. "OOOOOH," everyone gasped. It looked like a sure triple, but Luke Strohmer, our left fielder, made a spectacular running catch. Even Jasper looked up.

People screamed, jumped, and woo-hooed. "AWESOME CATCH!!" yelled Tank, practically in my ear. "Gold glove, dude!"

    Luke was one of the school's best athletes. He was always breezily rolling down the hall, accepting high fives, girls trailing after him.

    Now the whole stadium was cheering like crazy. I wondered if I should join in, but I didn't want to act like a dumb sports fan. I looked at Jasper.

    He had put away his comic book.

Whenever I caught a baseball game on TV, it droned on and on. But this one was different. There were stolen bases, diving catches, even a screaming argument at second base.

And then something amazing happened. The Silver Hawks were beating us 3-2, when our first baseman, Bruce "Bruiser" Pekarsky, came to bat. He hit a home run so far, it cleared the right-field bleachers and bounced off a car in the parking lot. Everyone's jaw dropped.

It was so cool, Jasper and I were both yelling as Bruiser crossed home plate. I didn't even mind the jocks behind us.

"Sweet!" they howled, bumping chests.

The air smelled like wet grass and root beer, and the mood was enjoyably tense. *I'm having a good time*, I realized with surprise.

After that, the Woodchucks were flying high. Heading into the ninth, we were leading 6-3. By coin flip, we were officially the home team, so we'd bat last. The way things were going, though, we probably wouldn't even need our final turn.

The crowd was going crazy. After twenty-five years of losing, the championship was just three measly outs away.

Three measly outs!

The game wasn't over yet, but people didn't care. They were already planning the

victory party, pouring soda on each other and
high-fiving.

Highland's first batter struck out.

"The Curse of the woodchucks is finished!"
Chantal shouted. "Dead! Gone! Six feet under!"

Their second batter grounded out to second.
One out to go...

"Hey, Highland!" Kyle yelled to the other
team. He turned around and pulled down his
pants.

Talk about Woodchuck Pride. Even Jasper laughed.

"One more out," someone whispered. "One more out..."

That's all it would take, and then the Woodchucks would be All-City Baseball Champs.

But then Dex Van Zandt walked up to the plate, the Silver Hawks' best hitter. Woodchuck fans groaned. The whole stadium held its breath as Dex fouled off two pitches.

"One more strike!" I burst out.

The pitcher wound up and threw. The batter swung. CRA-A-A-A-CK! The ball soared high above the third base line... reached its peak and started down... heading straight at us!

Two seconds later, I made the biggest mistake of my life.

* CHAPTER TWO *

The ball came arching down toward our section, closer and closer . . . right at me. If I didn't do something, it was going to conk me on the head! I put my hands up to catch it. Even though I reek at baseball, I thought I had this one — it was twenty feet away, ten, five, practically IN MY HANDS, and then —

WHAP!

The ball arrived just as Luke Strohmer's glove collided with my hand. He was reaching over the fence and into the stands, trying to make the catch. The ball dropped through my fingers and bounced at my feet.

"$%&*@*&%!" Luke roared.

He threw his glove to the ground and glared at me. Did I just block him from making the play? People started to boo.

Now he was swearing! I never even saw Luke coming — after all, I was looking up at the ball. In that split second, my only thought had been to stop the thing from bouncing off my head.

Holy crud.

"Foul ball," said the announcer, and the ump motioned for me to toss it back. I hesitated, shy about my throwing skills. Finally someone else picked it up and threw it onto the field.

The Silver Hawk hitter, Dex Van Zandt, smiled.

"Boooooooooooooo!" The crowd roared. "He should be out! That was Luke's ball!"

Tank poked me from behind. "You better hope Dex doesn't get a hit. Luke was totally going to catch that ball."

"This is YOUR fault!" hissed another guy.

Now it was starting to sink in that everyone was mad. Not just mad: _furious_.

But...but...!

It was totally unfair. All I'd done was stick my hands out when the ball came at me — that's what _everyone_ did! Luke had reached into the stands, right?

Or had I reached out onto the field?

Catching a ball in the stands was allowed. A fan reaching over the fence and onto the field was another story — that was illegal, wrong, and highly uncool. I was just protecting myself; I never meant to interfere with Luke. But it seemed the rest of the stadium saw it otherwise.

"You might've lost us the game, dirtbag," yelled someone else.

I sank into my seat, terrified. A moment later, I heard a loud _thunk_ of the bat and a big cheer went up on the Highland side.

Total disaster. I didn't even have to watch to know what happened. Dex Van Zandt had hit a home run.

Things only got worse.

The next Silver Hawk hit a triple. Then there were two walks in a row. Our outfielder dropped an easy fly ball. The woodchucks were giving up runs left and right, and all we could do was watch in horror.

The Silver Hawks tied the game and kept right on scoring:

6–6.

8–6.

11–6.

Even Jasper, who hated sports, looked crushed. "This is _pathetic_."

That foul ball had changed the whole momentum of the game. The Woodchucks had lost their confidence. The crowd groaned as Highland's worst hitter knocked a clean double. And then...

PLOP.

A half-open bag of peanuts landed in my lap. I brushed the bag away — maybe someone had dropped it by mistake. I tried to concentrate on the field.

THUNK.

Something wet hit my back. I reached behind me and found a half-empty soda can and put it on the floor. Crud! By the time I'd been pelted with a tube sock, a Big Gulp cup, and a magazine, I had to admit it wasn't an accident.

"Hope you're happy, jerkwad." I could feel one of the jocks poking me in the back.

"Moron!"

"IDIOT!"

I sat frozen in my seat, my heart pounding. Was this really happening? I stared straight ahead. Jasper leaned over and whispered, "Ignore them."

THWAP!

A meatball sub hit me in the neck and slid down the front of my jacket. Grimacing, I tried to wipe off the bits of meat and onion. I could hear the guys behind me laughing.

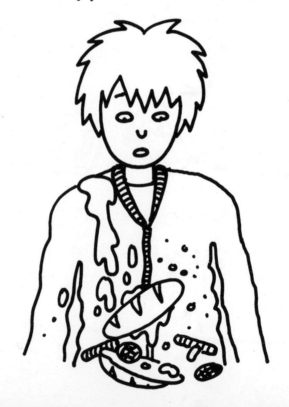

"Let's get out of here," I said to Jasper without looking at him. I pulled my head into my sweatshirt like a turtle.

"No." He looked around nervously. "You'd draw even more attention. Better stay till the game's over, then sneak out with the crowd."

I sank lower in my seat.

By the time the Woodchucks finally got the third out, we were down 12-6. We still had a chance — a _tiny_ chance — if we could put together a big rally in the bottom of the ninth. _Turn this thing around_, I prayed.

The first batter popped out to the shortstop.

The second batter hit a long fly ball . . . straight to the center fielder.

The third batter struck out in three pitches.

Noooooooooooooooooo!

   "And that's the game," trilled the announcer. "Let's hear it for the Silver Hawks" — a huge cheer from Highland — "the new All-City Baseball Champs!!!"

   Woodchuck fans wailed like they were at a funeral. I heard a jock behind me yell, "It's HIS fault!" and I turned around to see him pointing at me. "He ruined it! He jinxed the game!"

"LOSER! LOSER!" People were pointing.
The chant got louder. "LOSER! LOSER!
LOSER!"

Now fifteen hundred people were yelling
at me. My stomach felt like it had dropped to
my knees.

"Let's am-scray," said Jasper, pulling me out of my seat. "Put your collar up and —"

"LOSER! LOSER! LOSER!"

At least they don't know my name, I thought.

"HEY, DANNY!" Chantal yelled by megaphone.

Crud.

"WAS THAT YOU, DANNY? MESSING UP LUKE'S CATCH?" Now everyone was looking from me to Chantal. Since when did cheerleaders stop and talk to people in the stands?

"I THOUGHT YOU HATED SPORTS," she
shouted. "Dang."

I refused to look at her.

"DANNY SHINE!" she yelled. "Look at me
when I'm —"

A woman security guard in a blue uniform
tapped me on the shoulder. "I'll escort you out.
It's for your own safety."

For your own safety? Now I was even more worried. The security guard herded us through the crowd, down the stairs. As we passed the field, we saw an astonishing sight: hundreds of fans storming the field, throwing trash and yelling.

"SILVER HAWKS SUCK! SILVER HAWKS SUCK!"

And the strange thing was — it wasn't just hard-core jocks. Normal-looking girls were going crazy too, tearing up the grass, stomping on signs, and turning over garbage cans.

"This is insane," Jasper said.

The fans' rage scared me. Before, they'd cheered the team like crazy; now they were trashing the field with the same intensity. Like someone had flipped a switch.

"That Danny kid," said someone behind us. "His life is over."

Jasper and I froze.

"Go," said the security guard.

CHAPTER THREE

* TOP FIVE VOICEMAILS I DIDN'T WANT TO HEAR

1. "Hey, Danny! You owe me three dollars for the hot dog I threw at you!"
2. "It's Asia, just back from Wisconsin. How was the game?"
3. "Don't worry. We'll get another shot at the title in 2085."
4. "Jasper here. Want to borrow my Yoda Mask?"

5. "When you switch schools, can I have your locker?"

    The next day in school, I tunneled through the crowd, not speaking to anyone. A few people said things like, "Nice catch, dorkwad!" As soon as I got to homeroom, I shoved my nose in a book. I wanted to put the game out of my mind.

    Unfortunately, the principal brought it up in his PA announcement.

    "About the baseball championships." Dr. Kulbarsh sighed. "The Woodchucks played admirably and came very close to winning. Painfully close." He swallowed. "We were all disappointed. But I was even more disappointed in the fans' behavior after the game."

    A few people looked at the floor.

"Losing is no excuse to go on a rampage. You were guests at the stadium, and you abused the privilege. If that's how you behave, you don't deserve a team. In a time of budget cutbacks, the school must make painful choices. And that is why we are considering…" He paused dramatically. "Cutting after-school sports."

Everyone gasped.

I looked up from my book.

"We're reviewing the matter and will give you our decision in a few weeks," said Kulbarsh.

The knot in my stomach got bigger. It wasn't my fault the fans went crazy! But I sat glued to my desk, unable to look at anyone.

I'd always complained that sports got all the attention at this school. But not having them at all? That made even me feel weird. With a twinge, I remembered the game before the Incident. Sitting in the bleachers, the breeze on my face had felt good, and the game was strangely absorbing. It was hard to imagine it all going away.

"I bet he's just trying to scare us," a girl behind me said.

Maybe.

But just in case, I walked out of class with my head down.

"Look!" I heard Kyle, Tank's friend, behind me. "It's the guy who lost the game for us!"

WOODCHUCK SOCCER

CRUD! CRUD! DOUBLE CRUD!

This was the moment I'd been dreading. I tried to run the other way, but Tank blocked me.

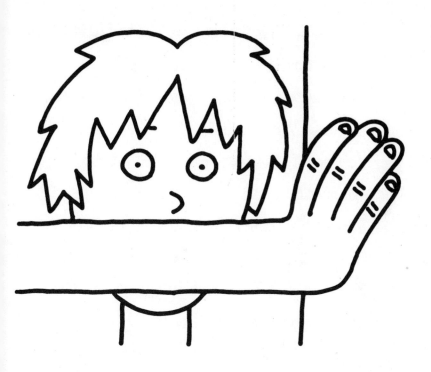

  "Traitors can't get through." He smiled lazily, like he had all the time in the world.

  More thick-necked guys came over.

  "Traitor!"

  "FREAK!"

  "You lost the game for us!"

  My heart was pounding like crazy. A crowd had gathered around us, hoping for a fight.

"I'm not a traitor, moron," I muttered under my breath.

Tank's eyes widened. "What did you say?"

I sighed. "Nothing."

"He's got to answer for what he did," Kyle announced.

"So." Abs, another jock, got in my face. "Why'd you ruin Luke's catch?"

"Yeah." Kyle poked me. "Why?"

Not sure if I should answer, I looked around for Jasper. He'd know what to do. I didn't see him, though, so I took a deep breath and said, "Look, I'll explain." I tried to keep my voice level.

The jocks pressed closer.

I took another deep breath. "When the ball came at me, I put my hands up to catch it. Everyone did. And if that's a crime, then..." I lifted my chin. "All the guys in my row were guilty."

"NAAAW!" Tank roared. "No one else knocked Luke out of the way. You blew it for him!"

"Maybe Luke blew it himself!" I yelled back.

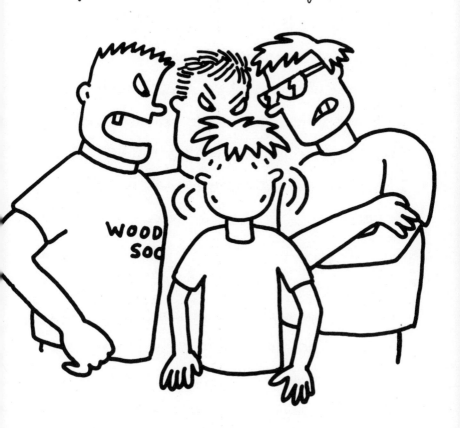

Tank looked like he was about to explode. He shut his eyes and blared like a foghorn.

"DON'T...EVER...DISS...THE LUKE."

Kyle pointed at me. "HE IS SO DEAD!!!"

"FIGHT! FIGHT! FIGHT!" people chanted.
The guys pushed me against a locker, and
suddenly I couldn't breathe. Don't barf, I
prayed, between waves of nausea.

"Bring him here!" Kyle pointed behind the
staircase. They dragged me across the floor,
eager to tear me limb from limb. The last thing
I saw was Tank twisting my arm and licking
his lips . . .

"Dawgs, what were you thinking?"

Tank, Kyle, Abs, two other jocks, and I were
sitting in Amundson's office. Amundson was our
pathetic, always-trying-to-be-cool vice principal.
He had pried us apart in the hall before they
had a chance to skin me alive.

"Fighting is NOT cool," he lectured. "Fighting is the OPPOSITE of cool."

The jocks and I looked at the floor.

"If you guys have a problem," he said, "you can always come to my office and kick it." Amundson liked to think he could relate to young people.

The jocks rolled their eyes.

"Who started it?" Amundson asked.

Looking at five muscle-bound giants and me,
it couldn't have been hard to figure out. But I
wasn't going to say anything. Then one of the
jocks mumbled something about "Danny ruining
the game."

Amundson turned to me with surprise. "That
was you?"

I nodded.

"I didn't even know you liked baseball,"
he said.

Boy, was I getting tired of hearing that.

"Now, hear this, dawgs." Amundson's voice got
rougher as he addressed the jocks. "You guys lay
off Danny. Cut the dude some slack."

At least I've got someone on my side, I
thought.

"He's not good at sports. He didn't know that
by getting in Luke's way, he'd blow our chance

at a championship. He had no idea his actions could bring down the whole sports program."

This was how he defended me?

"Promise you'll leave Danny alone," Amundson said.

The jocks grunted.

"Great," said Amundson. "It's settled."

Why did I get the feeling it wasn't?

We all stood up and shuffled out. Tank glared at me with a look that clearly said, "This isn't over."

* CHAPTER FOUR *

I didn't see the poster until third period. It was on the wall outside the gym.

"Good grief." Jasper tore the poster down and looked at it. "Is that your old yearbook picture?"

"Yeah." I took the paper from Jasper and ripped it to shreds. It made me appreciate how good I'd had it before, when no one knew my name. Being ignored was definitely underrated.

"Danny!!" someone shouted. "Did Luke kick your butt yet?"

"Loser!" another guy yelled.

"That's the one from the game who —" Two girls stopped whispering and stared.

Lunchtime was the worst.

It was the second school day after the Incident. I planned to just blend in — wait in line, get my three-cheese tuna melt, and make a beeline for our usual table. No eye contact, no conversation. There and back.

Inching forward in the lunch line, I kept my head in my book. I hoped wearing sunglasses would help. Unfortunately, the lenses were ultra-thick . . .

So I didn't see Tank's foot until it was too late.

WHAP! I fell to the floor, and my lunch splattered everywhere.

"HA HA HA HA HA." Laughter from the jocks' table rang in my ears. I picked the grilled cheese sandwich off the ground and brushed myself off, my hands shaking.

"Hey, Danny!" Tank yelled. "You forgot your sunglasses!" He swiped them off the floor and dangled them in the air. I decided not to reach for them.

"I've got a new name for you," his friend shouted. "The Sultan of Suck!"

Crud. Crud.

Double Crud.

Walking across the lunchroom, I was sweating like crazy.

Was this what school was going to be like from now on? It was bad enough that Jasper and I had to spend the morning tearing down WANTED posters. I went back to the lunch line for another sandwich.

I prayed this time I'd be ignored.

No such luck. Three seconds after I took my tray, someone threw me into a headlock. What now? I thought wearily. Looking down, I saw an arm with crude Sharpie tattoos on it. I groaned when I realized it was Axl, the school's worst bully.

Great, I thought. I get away from Tank, and now I'm up against Axl. Out of the frying pan, into the fire.

Without loosening his grip, Axl dragged me to the table with his pals Boris and Spike. The three of them formed the Skulls, Gerald Ford's only gang. Somehow I'd gotten suckered into drawing tattoos and graffiti for them when we were all in detention together, but we hadn't exactly become bosom buddies.

Axl   Boris   Spike

When I got to the table, I turned to Axl frantically. "I didn't push Luke out of the way!" I said. "I SWEAR! I didn't even see the guy until it was all over —"

"Oh, I don't care about the game." Axl spit a cherry pit into his napkin.

I swallowed. "You don't?"

Axl shrugged. "Nah. Baseball's dumb."

Oh, okay. Phew.

"It's not cool, like heli-skiing," Axl continued.

"Or parachuting off a radio tower," said Spike.

"Or cliff-diving," said Boris, chomping a giant chocolate chip cookie. Too bad Gerald Ford didn't offer any sports the Skulls considered manly enough.

"We don't care," Axl said. "None of us were even _at_ the game."

Okay. So...?

"I'm here to talk business." Axl leaned over. "I saw Tank trip you and the whole fight in the hall yesterday. Tank botched it. He should've just jumped you on the way home from school." Axl shook his head dismissively. "That's what _I_ would have done."

"I dunno." Spike frowned. "Torching someone's bike always sends a message."

Ha! Bullies critiquing each other's work. Who knew?

"These sports fans are insane," Axl said. "You think they're going to stop whaling on you? I'm offering an all-around protection package: lunchtime security, hallway defense, and locker surveillance."

"Protection package . . . ?"

"Anyone who writes graffiti, trashes your stuff, or wrecks your locker answers to us. Here's my card."

SKULLS SECURITY

Need someone beaten up?
"We Do It 4 u!"
Rush jobs no problem.

"H-how much does it cost?" I stammered.

"Twenty dollars a week for the standard package; thirty-five dollars for the deluxe. Deluxe includes after-school monitoring and an on-call alert system. It's an excellent value."

Wow. That was a lot of money.

I pretended to consider it. "I'll think it over."

"Sure. But if you <u>don't</u> do it . . ." Boris narrowed his eyes.

I looked up warily. "What?"

"We're going to be scraping you up..." Boris leaned toward me. "Off. The. Freakin'. Floor."

There was nothing like a good sales pitch.

* THINGS TO AVOID WHILE LYING LOW

The Bathroom

The Lunchroom

Chantal Davis

I devised a new hallway route that kept me away from Chantal and her gang. If I walked to the east annex staircase instead of the main one, I would miss her coming out of the bathroom after lunch. It worked.

Until one day I forgot and took the wrong stairs. When I heard Chantal & Co. rolling down the hall, I froze.

"Danny!" Chantal stopped dead when she saw me. Before I could escape, she cornered me against a locker. "You and me got issues. You lost us the game, and you know what that means? We didn't get to do our victory routine to the new Beyoncé song."

"It was slammin' too," said Raina. "We would have repeated it at Spirit Week, except —"

"We didn't have one," Da'Nise said flatly.

"And now we won't go to any regional championships." Chantal's voice was sad. "Where

you stay overnight at a hotel room and go to a fancy dinner. Order anything you want."

"I already had a dress picked out," said Raina.

I shifted uncomfortably. A crowd had gathered.

Kirby Hammer, a baseball player, came forward. "Right now I would have had a trophy in my room," he said quietly. "Maybe a championship ring."

"We could've marched in the Fourth of July parade," someone complained.

"And had a banner up at the mall," another guy said dreamily.

I could see my foul-up at the game had deprived everyone of something different — even if they were just fantasies.

Then I thought about what it had deprived me of: normal life.

* CHAPTER FIVE *

"Even if I barf?" said Sophie. "It'll be totally worth it."

She was talking about Da' Bomb, the new roller coaster, supposed to be the tallest, fastest, and scariest in North America. We were on the bus going to Mega-Fun amusement park, on the big class outing.

We'd all seen the ads:

The field trip was all anyone had talked about for weeks, and I wasn't going to miss it. I was ready to get back out in the world, eat greasy funnel cakes, and ride the Scrambler and Da' Bomb. It sure beat a normal Friday of Fun with Phonics, baked fish nuggets, and a cyber-safety assembly.

Tank and his gang would just have to deal with it.

"I'm looking forward to the food," I told Sophie. "There's nothing like a deep-fried Oreo . . ."

"Corn on a stick!" said my friend Emma.

"Two-foot hot dog!" said Morgan.

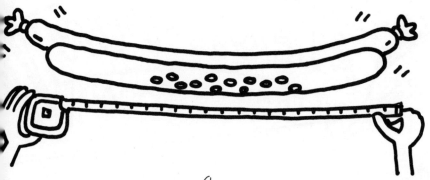

"I'm glad you came today, Danny," said Emma softly. "I hope those jerks don't bother you anymore."

"I can handle them," I said, in a burst of confidence. It helped that Tank and Luke were on another bus. Being with my friends again made me feel like I could do anything. I needed people more than I'd realized — to laugh at something I said or even tease me about being short. Other people remind you who you are, for better or worse.

Finally we saw the sign in the distance:

Everyone cheered. When we drove through
the gates, we crossed a moat and passed a
bunch of cool-looking rides.

Pouring out of the bus, Jasper and I headed
straight for Da' Bomb. The giant ride's loops,

dips, and dives stretched out in front of us like some exotic city.

We raced over to the ride's entrance and got in line. It was early in the day, so the line wasn't very long. In no time, Jasper and I were on the platform, ready to go. Just as a new set of roller-coaster cars rolled in, someone grabbed my arm.

It was Asia. "We can go up together!" she said, pointing to two empty seats.

We jumped in, and the operator shut the gate right after us. "The ride's closed!"

I looked back at Jasper, suddenly realizing he'd missed the cutoff. "Sorry!" I yelled. Chantal, Axl, and others glared at us; they'd have to wait too. Phil Petrokis and Kirby Hammer were in the car ahead of us; we were the only four from school who got on.

"That's not fair!" grumbled Chantal.
Everyone wanted to be first on the ride.

As Asia and I sank into our seats, giant safety straps pressed down on us. My heart started to pound. Three thousand feet of intense drops, I'd heard. What if I got dizzy or freaked out or barfed on the coolest, most beautiful girl at Gerald Ford?

"You look a little pale," Asia said. "Are you scared?"

"Scared! Of this thing?" I looked up at the five-story drop and swallowed. "Hardly."

The car inched upward on the track with a loud cranking sound, every second bringing us closer to the top and making me more and more tense.

Up, up, up.

Looking below us, I broke into a sweat.
What had I done? <u>Did I really need to go on
the scariest ride ever with a girl I was trying
to impress?</u>

Crud!

Now we were almost at the edge of the giant
drop. From that height, we could see the whole
park, a maze of highways, and the city in the
distance. We were pulling closer to the drop,
now just a few feet away. I tried to prepare
myself.

Only inches to go . . . YIKES! We were almost over the edge, and then —

We stopped.

Huh?

Asia and I looked at each other. "What's going on?" she asked. "Something's wrong."

We waited. And waited.

Still — nothing. We looked back behind us — we were at the very top of the roller coaster!

"ATTENTION, RIDERS. THERE HAS BEEN A TECHNICAL MALFUNCTION," said a voice coming from the loudspeaker. "THE IMPORTANT THING IS NOT TO PANIC."

When someone tells you not to panic, what's the first thing you do?

Panic.

* FIVE THINGS YOU DON'T WANT TO HEAR ON TOP OF A ROLLER COASTER

1. "Look at all the ambulances..."
2. "Sorry — management wouldn't spend extra for brakes."
3. "Accident-free for five days!"
4. "This ride has an 80 percent survival rate."
5. "Houston, we have a problem."

Now I was scared out of my mind. But as the minutes ticked by, I worried less about falling and more about what to say to Asia. I hadn't planned on any more conversation than "whew — that was scary!" or "Skittles?"

What did I talk about with Jasper? None of our debate topics seemed right: Best James Bond: Connery or Brosnan? Worst job: leech farmer or butt doctor? Is it better to have freeze vision or invisibility?

But then Asia said something, and I said something back. Time started to just go by. It wasn't as hard as I thought.

* ASIA O'NEILL: RANDOM FACTS

Secretly cries at phone commercials

Has a dog named Milkshake

Wishes school had a badminton team

Doesn't believe in suntans

Wants to design all-female video games

I found myself telling her things, like my idea for a perfume that smells like new art supplies. Asia laughed. "I like talking to you, Danny," she said. "You're not afraid to have weird ideas."

A compliment, sort of. "Thanks."

"I appreciate that because I'M weird," she said. "I don't like girly stuff like cheerleading and shoe sales. I'd rather be playing Garage Band."

"Yeah?" She really was the coolest. "I love Garage Band."

"Yeah?" she said.

"Yeah." Did I dare? "Maybe some time we could —"

"ATTENTION, RIDERS," the loudspeaker voice blared. Crud! Now they had to make an announcement?

"WE'LL BE EVACUATING EVERYONE STARTING NOW. THANKS FOR YOUR PATIENCE."

Talk about bad timing.

"Woo-hoo!" Asia raised her fist in the air. "We're getting out of here!"

"Great," I said glumly.

The roller coaster started moving again, chugging slowly backward. When our feet finally touched the ground, all the Gerald Ford kids were waiting for us.

"Thank God you're safe," said Mrs. Lacewell, the school administrator.

But our classmates looked downright angry.

"They're shutting down the ride," said Axl. "That reeks."

"S'not fair!" cried Chantal.

"Hey, Danny!" Jasper called out.

"Wait a minute!" Tank pushed through the crowd and poked a finger into my chest. "You were on the ride?"

Everyone got quiet.

I swallowed. "Yeah. So?"

"Well." Tank threw up his hands. "That explains it. He went up there, and the thing DIED! He's a jinx!"

"That's ridiculous," Asia said, scowling at Tank.

"No, Tank's right," said Chantal. "He IS a jinx."

Give me a break!

"Phil and Kirby were there too," I protested.

"Yeah, but —" Tank grinned. "They don't have your track record."

Excitement ran through the crowd.

"Ha ha!" A girl shouted. "Danny's a jinx!"

Other kids picked up on it. "JINX! JINX! JINX! JINX!"

The stalled ride was being blamed on me?

Good grief.

"You think I wanted to be stuck up there?" My voice was frantic.

"Doesn't matter," said Tank. "Look at your backpack."

I frantically tried to rub it out.

"The ink's permanent," someone said.

* CHAPTER SIX *

Here's the thing about middle school: The truth doesn't matter. Once a rumor gets started, it stays in people's minds. When the real story comes out, it's too late — you've already been branded.

* A FEW UNTRUE RUMORS AT GERALD FORD:

1. Someone's hamburger had a tail.
2. Pinky Shroeder took his mother to prom.
3. When Principal Kulbarsh wants time alone, he pulls the fire alarm.

4. Ethan Fogerty barfed up a live worm.

5. Danny Shine broke the roller coaster just by sitting in it.

After the Roller Coaster Disaster, basically everything that went wrong at the school was my fault.

If someone flunked a quiz...

If someone fell off his scooter . . .

If a doorknob came off in someone's hand . . .

I got blamed.

They even said I caused a rainstorm. "Hurricane Danny" came one afternoon, wiping out a day of relay races. Walking home the next day, Jasper tried to make me feel better.

"It's getting ridiculous," he said. "No one can seriously think you caused this stuff. I mean, the Biology rabbit got cancer. How is that your fault? And Bruiser Pekarsky's the one who bent the basketball rim."

"I couldn't reach that thing on a bet," I said.

"They're just blame-shifting," Jasper said. "It's not fair."

We passed by the park, and I planted myself on one of the benches overlooking a pond. For a few minutes, neither of us said anything.

"Homeschooling is starting to sound like a good idea," I said.

"WHAT?" Jasper stood up and stared at me. "Don't say that!"

"But I have to do <u>something</u>..." I said. Being at school was getting weirder and weirder.

* HOMESCHOOLING: THE PROS AND CONS

PRO: Relaxed dress code

CON: Boring yearbook

PRO: Shoo-in for class
president.

CON: Low attendance at
school dances.

"If you left school," Jasper gasped, "it would
be horrible. Who would I play Boggle with? Who'd
get my Rat Girl references? Or argue with me
about dubbing versus subtitles?"

I was flattered by his reaction. I'd feel
the same way if he suddenly told me he was
going to Science Genius Academy.

"Thanks," I said. "Don't worry, I'm not going anywhere."

At least, not yet.

The next day, Jasper and I walked to the auditorium to get our pictures taken. You could tell it was Photo Day because no one was wearing cutoff shorts or a T-shirt that said "Compost Happens." All food fights and butt-kickings had been postponed for a day. Even Axl was quietly reading an army supply catalog.

Grooming products were everywhere.

Chantal passed by, wheeling a clothing rack. "What's this?" I asked.

"You're supposed to bring an extra outfit." Chantal's voice was impatient. "Didn't you read the handout?"

Yeah, but — it looked like she'd brought about ten. Stopping by the drinking fountain, Jasper and I saw Ginnifer Baxter and Katelyn Ogleby, best friends who refused to admit they were separate people. They were both wearing elaborate hairdos with combs, barrettes, and even flowers woven in.

"How are my bangs?" I heard Ginnifer ask Katelyn. "Too much product?"

"Here." Katelyn licked her finger and adjusted one of Ginnifer's strands. "That's better. How about me?"

"Almost," Ginnifer said. "Blot your lip balm."

"Finger-fluff your curls in back."

"Sweater lint alert!"

For some people, Photo Day was a big deal.

How had I

prepared? By looking in the mirror to make sure I wasn't paint-splattered or bleeding. Jasper's indifference went a step further.

Approaching the auditorium, I couldn't help asking, "You did <u>know</u> it was Photo Day, right?"

"Sure," said Jasper, taking another gulp of his Yoo-hoo. "But why should I comb my hair just to impress people?"

Outside the auditorium, we went to the back of the line, which stretched out to the school's main double doors. There were at least fifty people ahead of us.

"WAAAAAAAAAAAAAAAAAAAAAAAAAAH!"

We heard screaming from inside. A second later, Sophie burst out of the auditorium. "The sprinkler went off in the cafeteria!" she said. "Ralph was fixing it, and the valve released.

All these girls got drenched — in their fancy clothes!"

My first reaction was relief. At least this was one incident that could not — by any stretch of the imagination — be blamed on me. Then I felt bad for Ralph, who had never been a very good janitor.

Later that day, I went by the supply closet to see how Ralph was doing. I also wanted to tell him about some goofball who'd written "JINX" in mustard all over our lunch table.

"Hey, Ralph." I kicked the door open, not bothering to knock. "You won't believe the latest —"

Ralph was slumped on a bucket of barf powder, reading a comic I'd lent him.

"Not now, Danny." Ralph held up his hand. "I've got my own problems. This comic of yours got me into big trouble! It was so funny, I stopped to read it while fixing the sprinkler. Before I knew it, the valve released. What a mess."

I stared at him. "My comic . . . ?"

"Never give me stuff when I'm working," he said. "You know how distracted I get!"

My brain slowly took it in. I was linked to the disaster after all. Starting the day, I'd felt unfairly blamed. But now I began to wonder.

Could everyone have been right?

"Danny? Are you okay?" asked Ralph.

"Yeah, I just — have to go." I bolted for the door, needing time to think.

Out in the hall, someone called out, "HEY, JINX!" This morning I would have been really annoyed.

Now, I sort of believed it too.

* CHAPTER SEVEN *

"Jinx, shminx," said Logan. I was hanging out at Comix Nation, trying to avoid people from school. Sitting on a stool by the counter, I breathed in the comforting smell of stale bubble gum and old comic books. Logan, the owner, was snarfing down her usual four-o'clock Taco Dog lunch special.

CHOMP CHOMP

"I mean, it's flattering to think you have the power to get people in trouble." Logan drained a cup of soda. "But it's delusional — like believing you're Superman or Rat Girl. Except instead of having X-ray vision, you think you can stop roller coasters. Well, I got news for you." She poked a finger in my chest. "You can't."

I half-smiled. Logan had a way of making you get over yourself. But she didn't know how it felt to get made fun of all day long.

Logan handed me a bit of taco to feed to her dog, General Zod, who was panting at my feet. I reached down. He swallowed it greedily and licked his lips. His doggy breath felt good against my hand.

"So what else is bugging you?" asked Logan.

I kicked the counter. "Tomorrow we start this dumb public-speaking project," I said. "Every seventh grader has to write and deliver a five-minute speech."

"That's not so bad." Logan unwrapped a candy bar.

It _was_ bad. The part I dreaded most was getting assigned a coaching partner. Who would want to be with a known jinx? But to Logan, I just said, "What am I going to talk about?"

"Danny." Logan pointed toward the stacks. "Look around. There's topics all over the store! Comic books have so many great ideas in 'em, it's not even funny."

My mind was blank. "Like . . . what?"

"Like what?" Logan slammed down her soda cup so hard, General Zod gave a startled bark. "Like — how can power be used in the best way?

When is hurting people justified? How can you turn a traumatic experience into something positive?" She pointed to some nearby comics.

"Hmmm." Maybe.

"You could even talk about that horrible baseball game." Logan lifted her chin in a dare. "What you learned from it."

My chest tightened. "I didn't learn anything."

"Come on." Logan scowled. "Lots of comic book characters have a past that haunts them — a radioactive accident or the death of a family member. They move on and, you know" — Logan coughed, and shifted on her stool — "Accept themselves."

I've done that, I thought. I've accepted that I'm a jinx.

"You'll think of something. In the meantime . . ." She lifted a box of comic books from behind the counter. "Here. Make your lazy self useful."

I sighed like it was a chore. But
I was happy to have somewhere to be, with
General Zod at my feet, gnawing my sneakers.

＊　　＊　　＊

Our English teacher, Mrs. Wagman, stood in front of the class like an army commander. She waited for everyone to quiet down so she could announce partners for the public-speaking project.

"I don't want to hear any whining," she said. "The matchups are _completely random_ —

done by computer. And don't ask if you can be reassigned. The answer is NO."

Everybody groaned.

"What if I get someone I don't like?" asked Sophie.

"What if I get someone who's a dork?" asked Tank.

"What if I get Axl?" asked Raina.

"It's not a date for the school dance," Wagman said with a sigh. "It's a coaching partner. You read each other's speeches and make suggestions. The point is to help each other."

"And this year, we have a special opportunity," confided Wagman. "Five of you will be chosen by the class to give a speech at assembly . . . TO THE PRINCIPAL HIMSELF!" She said it like she was announcing a surprise pizza party.

Silence.

"People," she went on, lowering her voice. "If you're picked, you can tell Dr. Kulbarsh anything you want. This is your big chance. Any ideas?"

Silence again.

Finally, Pinky Shroeder raised his hand. "In gym, they should teach minigolf."

"We should get school off for Valentine's Day," said Ginnifer Baxter.

"Full-page yearbook photos," said Chantal.

"Hmmm. Well." Mrs. Wagman raised her eyebrows. "If that's what you're passionate about."

"Tell us our partners already!" someone yelled out.

I felt a wave of dread. All around me, girls were buzzing about who would get paired with Luke Strohmer. Tossing around a mini basketball, he seemed unaware of the stir he was causing. Were there any downsides to being a good-looking, popular jock?

* TOP FIVE DOWNSIDES TO BEING LUKE STROHMER

1. Sore hand from accepting high fives
2. All those boring sports award dinners
3. Your phone's overloaded with numbers

4. Can't pick your nose with all eyes on you

5. Never know if you're liked for yourself or
   your ripped abs

   "Okay, everyone," Wagman said. "I'm going to
read the partner assignments. No booing."

   She went down the list: Angie Bilandic —
Jason Hofstaeder. Da'Nise Freemont — Morgan
Chatterjee. "Axl Ryan," Wagman said, and
everyone held their breath. "Chantal Davis."

"AXL RYAN?" Chantal yelled, eyes wide in disbelief. "No way! I refuse!"

Everyone buzzed excitedly. Axl and Chantal were coaching partners? Now _that_ was entertaining! The two of them were known rivals. They were the two most feared people in school, and the only ones not scared of each other.

Axl had been quietly whittling a skull into his desk with a pen knife.

But now he stood up. "Chantal can't turn me down," he said. "I'M turning HER down!"

"I said it first!" howled Chantal.

"Axl, Chantal, you'll just have to learn to get along," said Wagman. "No reassignments."

"Butthead," Chantal hissed at Axl.

"Big mouth," Axl muttered back.

Wagman started reading the names off faster now, to leave less time for a reaction. Jasper got Velvet Stern, a major airhead.

Finally, my name. "Danny Shine." Wagman paused, and I held my breath.

"Who're you going to jinx _this_ time?" Kyle shouted. The class cracked up.

"I'm glad he can't ruin _my_ speech!" roared Chantal.

Everyone leaned forward, excited to find out. Wagman clutched her piece of paper and swallowed.

"Luke Strohmer," she said.

* CHAPTER EIGHT *

"OOOOOOOOOOOOOOOOOOOOOOOOOO
OOOOH!" The class exploded.

Luke's face turned beet red.

HE was my new partner?

Holy crud!

I'd been avoiding Luke like crazy. In the
hall, I always looked for his blue baseball cap,
and if I saw it, I dove to the side. My personal
"Luke-dar" told me where he was at all times —
laughing with a bunch of jocks, whipping a towel
at someone in the locker room, skateboarding
down the street. I made sure to stay away.

Now we were stuck together. And today, of all days, he'd taken the seat right in front of me.

The class could barely contain its excitement. This was a thousand times <u>better</u> than Axl and Chantal — like having a reality show right here in school! Everybody started talking at once.

"DANGER ISLAND"

"Too bad about Luke," Jasper said to me. He looked over at his new partner. "Being with Velvet will be, uh, interesting. She'll teach me about fashion, and I'll teach her about astrophysics."

Is this outfit too matchy-matchy?

Meanwhile, Luke scowled and kicked the chair legs in front of him with his sneaker. I sank lower in my seat and pretended to be absorbed in a book.

"Settle down, people," said Wagman. "For the rest of class, you can get to know your partner."

Tank stood up. "Can I just say something?" He didn't wait for an answer. "Luke working with Danny — that's just _wrong_."

"S'not fair," Abs agreed. "Danny'll jinx him. Luke's a great speaker. Remember the talk he gave in the dugout before semifinals?"

"He, totally, like, inspired us," said Bruiser Pekarsky.

Luke looked at the floor.

"Luke! Luke! Luke! Luke!" a few of the jocks started chanting.

Wagman's arms were folded, and she was frowning. But people continued to chant, "Luke!" as if they could change her mind. What did they expect Wagman to say? "Keep shouting, and I'll reconsider"?

"Enough," Wagman said in her this-discussion-is-over voice. "Everyone go talk to your partners. Luke, that includes you and Danny."

Luke tipped his chair back and looked at the ceiling. He did some air drumming on his desk. He unwrapped a gumball and stuck it in his mouth, rotating it from cheek to cheek. His stubbornness was impressive.

I waited, and finally, he spoke.

"You know, Wagman can't _make_ us be partners," Luke said bluntly. "We could both refuse."

"We could." I shrugged. "But what's the point? We'd get dragged to the office to 'kick it' with Amundson. He'd offer us caramel corn and say, 'Dawgs, I'm just not down with that.' We'd have to listen to his lecture about 'changing our 'tudes,' wishing we were home playing Call of Duty. And we'd _still_ have to be partners."

"Ha." Luke snorted. "I guess you know the drill."

"Yeah."

Luke lifted his chin. "Why were you at the baseball game, anyway? I see you more at, like, Mathletes or French Club," he said. "Type of guy who gets allergy shots and goes to Biology Camp."

Ouch! I was hoping I came across as more normal and less like president of the Insect Club.

"I went to the game 'cause I wanted to."
I squirmed in my chair.

Luke shook his head. "I've seen that play in my head a thousand times. The ball flies over third base. I stretch my arm into the stands. I catch it. We win the game."

"Huh."

"Then my parents take me to the Steak House."

"I have the same dream." I lowered my voice. "I'm in the stands, but I don't raise my arms. I just let the ball head straight for me. Then you catch it and everyone's happy."

"Hmmm." Luke frowned.

"I wish it had happened like that," I said. "Since then, my life has been dog barf."

"Your life?" Luke kicked the floor angrily. "How about mine? If I'd made the play, we might have won the championship. You think that's easy to live with?"

"Maybe we both messed up." I shrugged.

"How did I mess up?" Luke stood up. "You got in my way. They should have called fan interference!"

I stood up too and glared back. "I didn't reach onto the field! I was just trying to protect myself and not get hit!"

Mrs. Wagman broke in with an announcement. "By Friday, you have to have the topic sentence and first paragraph of your speech written. So arrange with your partner to get together after school and work on it — at your house or their house!"

Me at Luke's house?

Yeeesh.

"And did I mention?" Wagman said sweetly.

"The speech counts for half your grade."

Luke buried his head in his hands.

"That reeks," he muttered.

For once, I agreed with him.

* CHAPTER NINE *

Two days later, Luke opened the door of his house and glared. "Don't expect Oreos and Comedy Central," he said. "This is just business."

Nice to see you too, Luke. I stepped into his house and followed him to a family room with a long couch. Above the fireplace was a wall of trophies.

I picked one up, feeling the weight of it. What would it be like to have a whole shelf of these? Or even one?

"Some of those are my brothers'," he admitted. "Tripp plays varsity football. Gavin's state-ranked in tennis."

"Huh." A family of sports stars.

Luke's sister walked into the room with a bowl of popcorn. "Want some?" she offered. "I just microwaved it."

"No," Luke answered for both of us. "We're going to my room."

I followed him down the hall to a bedroom crammed with Chicago sports souvenirs — pennants, posters, framed baseball cards. I saw a life-size poster of T-Rex (Tyrell Rex Harris), the Cubs' new star hitter.

"You a fan?" I pointed to T-Rex.

"Yeah." Luke's face lit up. "He's awesome. And a great guy too — he coaches a group of —" He stopped abruptly. As if he suddenly remembered who I was, his jaw tightened.

I coughed politely. "Might as well get started." I sank into a beanbag chair and took out my speech. We were each supposed to have a topic sentence and first paragraph written.

"I can't work on an empty stomach," Luke announced, escaping down the hall. He returned with a bag of chips, which he didn't offer to share.

His phone pinged. "Angie again," he said, rolling his eyes. I nodded, as if getting too many texts from girls was a problem I could relate to.

"Got your speech?" I asked.

"My speech. Right." Luke reached for his backpack and stuck his arm in. He pulled out bandage tape, gym shorts, and a towel. Putting his arm in again, he pulled out a crumpled piece of paper from the bottom.

Why did I get the feeling this assignment was _not_ Luke's top priority?

"Okay," I said. "Let 'er rip."

"I just have to look something up." Luke typed into his computer. I figured he was checking a fact for his speech. "Nooo!" he wailed. "Tomorrow's salmon loaf."

"Luke . . . ?" I was irritated.

"Do yours first." He flopped on the bed, punching pillows.

I tried to sit up straight. It was hard to command authority from a beanbag chair.

"'Why the School Needs Better Pencil Sharpeners.'" Not wanting to attract attention, I picked the most boring topic I could think of.

After weeks of being the Jinx, I wanted people to forget me.

Silence.

I cleared my throat. "So many good pencils have been chewed up..."

Luke just stared out the window while I read my speech.

Finally, it was his turn. First, he had to watch game highlights on the Internet, change sweatshirts, and retape a hockey stick. When he couldn't put it off any longer, he slumped in his desk chair and stared at his speech, as if wondering how it got there.

"'Why Gerald Ford Needs After-School Sports,'" said Luke.

"Good title." Leaning back, I felt relieved. Now I'd find out if Luke was as good a speaker as his friends said.

I nodded for him to go ahead.

"'Why Gerald Ford Needs After-School Sports,'" he said in a hollow, zombie voice, staring straight ahead. "Sports and Gerald Ford..." he began, and then stopped.

"Luke...?" I asked.

He started the speech again. "S-sports and Gerald Ford," he stammered, "go together like a hot dog and mustard. Gerald Ford needs sports teams so we can kick Highland's butt."

I motioned for him to keep going.

"Sports is also, like, good exercise," he said. "And fans like games because they're free. They can see their friends win and enemies get creamed. Plus we already have team sweatshirts and hats and everything. So the easiest thing is just to keep playing. THE END."

I was quiet for a moment.

"Interesting." I figured it's always good to be positive. "Can I, uh, ask you something? What was the big speech you made in the dugout?"

"About victory among friends?" His face reddened. "I stole it from a gladiator movie on Showtime. Those weren't my words."

"Oh." This was bad news.

"Anyway, that was the dugout," said Luke. "If I had to do it at assembly? I'd puke."

"Don't worry," I chuckled. No way would he get picked to do his speech at assembly! We just had to get him through the in-class ordeal. "So, besides exercise, what do you get out of baseball?"

"I dunno," Luke snorted. "What do you get out of French Club?"

I gritted my teeth. "I'm not _in_ French Club. I'm just trying to help you out."

Luke frowned. "All right, let me think. Um . . ."

Finally, I thought, _He's settling down to work . . ._

Just then we heard a rumbling noise coming from the sidewalk outside. Luke peered out the window.

"WOO-HOO!!!!!!!!" he shouted, and ran out of the room.

When we got outside, my stomach sank. Skateboarders were circling on the street: Tank, Abs, and Kyle.

Tank came straight at me. He was about to run me over, then stopped with an inch to spare. He flipped the board up with his foot. "Don't tell me we're busting up a study session!"

Luke ducked his head, embarrassed. "We were pretty much done."

Done? We'd barely started!

"Luke doesn't need to practice," Tank said.

"He's a pro," said Abs. "You've should've heard his speech —"

"In the dugout, I know — Hey, wait a sec." It suddenly dawned on me. "You're not on the team. How did you hear it?"

"I didn't hear it," said Tank. "I heard about it."

"Me too," said Kyle.

Uh-oh. Kids who weren't even there were spreading the word. They'd built him up to be Abe Lincoln, Winston Churchill, and Nelson Mandela rolled into one.

And if he didn't deliver, guess who they'd blame?

* CHECK ONE

☐ His teacher
☐ His baseball coach
☐ Me

* CHAPTER TEN *

"Who wants to go first?" asked Mrs. Wagman.

Silence.

Today was the day we were supposed to give our speeches so the class could vote for the five best ones. Luke was seated in the back, tossing a mini basketball. It had been a week since we'd coached each other. I looked down at my speech nervously.

"Five of you will get picked to speak at assembly," Wagman said. "Pay attention, so you can vote. Now who wants to go first?"

Amazingly, Axl stood up.

"I'm ready," he said.

Wagman looked at him suspiciously. "Really?"

"Yeah."

"Um, okay, great," she said uncertainly.
"Come up front."

Spike and Boris followed Axl, flanking him
like Secret Service agents.

"Sit down," Wagman commanded, but they
didn't budge.

Finally, Axl nodded, and they went back to their seats.

"'If I Was Principal,'" said Axl, adjusting his do-rag.

Everyone giggled.

"There are a lot of wacked-out rules at school," said Axl. "Like how you're not supposed to keep roadkill in your locker."

"You can't 'borrow' someone's bike, even for a quick ride," he continued. "Or watch TV in class."

Boris nodded.

"I'd change that," said Axl. "Other things too. In gym, we'd learn kung fu, not kickball. Art teachers would teach tattoo-drawing. And the detention room would have a foosball table."

* AXL'S DREAM DETENTION ROOM

Axl went on to suggest better field trips ("A casino would be cool.") and that math should be optional. A few people cheered.

"You should run for student council," said Wagman.

"Can't." Axl shook his head. "Skulls meet after school," he explained, like it was Debate Club. As he walked back to his seat, someone high-fived him. It was Chantal!

Hearing surprised murmurs, Chantal turned around. "That's right. He did good! Thanks to _my_ coaching."

Wagman smiled. "Coaches can have a big effect on speeches."

Uh-oh, I thought.

Wagman smiled again. "Who's next? Hands?"

Kendra Maxtone-Cousins's arm shot up, and she marched to the front of the class. She was

the kind of student who organizes the Teacher-
Appreciation Breakfast.

Kendra smiled and began, "My speech is
called 'Why the School Day Should be Extended
Fifteen Minutes.'"

People started to throw things.

"HEY!" Wagman's voice was sharp. "You know the rules: no booing, throwing, or vomit noises."

Kendra finished her speech over a low hum of groans and sighs from the class. I was definitely NOT voting for Kendra.

Finally, it was my turn. I cleared my throat and began. "'Why the School Needs Better Pencil Sharpeners.'"

Q: How boring was my speech?

A: It was so boring, the school statue got up and left.

OUR FOUNDER

I felt stupid rambling on ("You can barely get a usable pencil point . . ."). My topic was a cop-out, but I wanted to be forgettable. If I put people to sleep, at least they wouldn't yell out, "Hey, Jinx!"

* FIVE SPEECHES THE PRINCIPAL DOESN'T WANT TO HEAR

1. Spelling: Will We Ever Use It in Real Life?

2. The Art of the Swirly
3. Cherry Bombs v. M-80s
4. Never Copy from Someone Dumber than You
5. Angie Bilandic: Hot or Not?

Finally, everyone had given their speech except one person.

"Luke?" called Mrs. Wagman. "You're up!"

Luke dragged himself to the front like he was going to prison. When he reached into his back pocket, I recognized the same crumpled-up piece of notebook paper I'd seen before.

"Luke! Luke! Luke!" the class chanted.

"Um, hey." Luke held out the crumpled paper. As he tossed his hair back, you could hear sighs from every girl in the room.

"My speech is..." Luke coughed and swallowed a few times. "'Why Gerald Ford Needs After-School Sports.'"

"Woo! Woo!!" The cheers were already beginning, and Luke hadn't even started the actual speech. His jock buddies were whistling and clapping. Mrs. Wagman's glasses slipped down her nose as she watched the class go wild.

"Shhhhhh!" said Mrs. Wagman. "Let's hear the speech."

Luke cleared his throat again. "S-sports and Gerald Ford," he stammered, "go together like a hot dog and mustard. Gerald Ford —"

"Yesssssssssssssssssss! Luuuuuuuuuuuuuuuke!" the class yelled.

"People...!" Wagman protested.

Droplets of sweat glistened on Luke's forehead. "Let's hear it for the Woodchucks,"

he said. Immediately, Tank started singing the
school fight song:

Ge-rald Fo-ord, we will fight for you
For the right to do
Everything for you . . .

Luke joined in, in a hoarse voice, and
then everyone was singing and shouting the words:

We'll go in to play and win the game
We will bring you fame! Rah! Rah! Rah!

Luke's speech had turned into a pep rally. His speech dropped to the floor, but he didn't seem to notice.

"GO, WOODCHUCKS!" Chantal ran up to the front of the class and started cheerleading. "Save after-school sports!"

The class roared, giving Luke a standing ovation even though he'd barely said a word. Jasper and I reluctantly got to our feet too.

"Now, Luke," said Wagman sternly. "That's fine, but that's not the assignment. You'll have to give a real speech. Start over, from the top."

But before Luke could start again, the bell rang.

The next day in class, Jasper handed Mrs. Wagman an envelope. He was the official vote counter.

"Here it is!" Wagman said, tearing it open. "These are the winners you picked to speak at assembly!" Wagman excitedly pulled out the card inside and stared at it.

Everyone waited.

"This can't be right," she said finally.

"Who? Tell us!" The class shouted out.

"It says —" Wagman shook her head. "Pinky Shroeder, Jenna Kerkorian, B. D. Sanchez, Maya Nevins, and, um — Luke Strohmer."

"Luke! Yay!" people cheered.

Wagman's brow furrowed. "Luke didn't give a speech," Wagman protested. "He doesn't qualify."

But the class started chanting:

Wagman sighed and went over to Jasper, who had tallied up the votes. After they'd talked for a few minutes, she came back.

"Okay." Wagman sounded resigned. "You voted for him. But, Luke, you're going to have to get serious. And Danny, as his coach, you have a LOT of work to do."

Great, I thought. Like I can get Luke to do anything.

Luke put on his lazy grin, but his face had turned a shade whiter.

When class was over, I whispered to Jasper as we walked out, "I still can't believe Luke won."

"Hey, Jinx." Tank had overheard me, and he pulled me aside. "I want to tell you something."

Jasper backed away, leaving us alone. Tank grabbed my shirt and pushed me against a locker.

"Luke's speech needs to be awesome — BETTER than awesome." Tank's voice was low. "Anything less, and I'm holding you responsible."

"Tank." I gulped. "He's not a very good speaker. He's —"

"Great." Tank's teeth were gritted. "Luke is great. He's going to change the principal's mind."

"But —"

"If you jinx this one, you're dead," he said. "Plain and simple."

"Tank —" I said, my voice pleading.

"You think you had it rough before?" Tank laughed. "You ain't seen nothing yet."

Luke sailed out of class with a bunch of friends slapping his back. I felt sick to my stomach.

* CHAPTER ELEVEN *

<u>If you jinx this one, you're dead.</u>

Tank's words kept running through my mind as I fidgeted in math class. I had to get Luke to work his butt off and ace the speech. In other words, pull off a freakin' miracle. When the bell rang, I bolted out of class and raced to Jasper's locker. Maybe he'd have some ideas.

But Jasper wasn't there. Impatiently, I looked around, asking if anyone had seen him. A girl overheard me and said, "He's at a Fashion Club meeting."

"FASHION CLUB?" I almost fell over.

Holy crud.

I ran to the Multi-Purpose Room. Jasper was

sitting at a table, working at his laptop. On the other end sat a bunch of overdressed girls. They stared at me as I came in.

"Jasper!" I whispered. "What are you doing here?"

He looked up, startled. "Velvet's about to give a presentation," he said.

"On what?"

Jasper's face reddened. "The Perfect Prom Hairstyle."

Geez.

"I'm just helping," Jasper said quickly. "She's been teaching me about fashion. It's more scientific than you'd think — how colors and fabrics go together."

"Huh." I didn't know what to say.

"It's a thought system I was unfamiliar with." Jasper stroked his chin like a professor.

That's when I noticed something alarming. For the first time since I'd known him, his sneakers weren't mismatched. In fact, they were brand-new basketball shoes, the latest model, the kind jocks wore.

Jasper! In trendy sneakers!

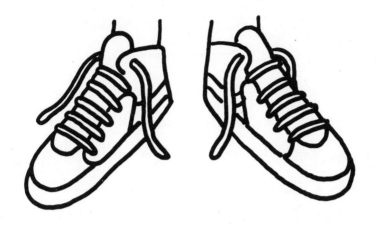

I felt pain in my chest. Where was the old Jasper, who wore mismatched shoes and thought Fashion Club was a joke?

"Why are you here?" Jasper pulled a seat up for me. "The next topic is 'Swimsuits for a Problem Body.'"

I tore my eyes away from Jasper's feet. "Look, I need to make Luke's speech really pop," I said. "Any suggestions?"

"Ummm . . ." Jasper's eyes strayed toward the computer screen. "Not really."

My chest sank. "Nothing?"

"Well, I —" Jasper typed something. "Sorry, my mind is on this PowerPoint thing."

"PowerPoint?"

"Yeah, I made all these cool charts and graphs. See?" He brought up images on the screen. "Visual stuff really helps. Like, here's a graph about matching your shape to different swimsuit styles."

That was it! The idea I was waiting for!

"PowerPoint would be great for Luke," I said. "He could show statistics about school sports."

A moment later, I was engulfed in a cloud of fruity perfume. "Did you just mention Luke?" asked Kiki DeFranco.

The rest of the girls stopped talking.

"Yeah," I said. "I'm helping him with his speech."

"Luke needs help?" Ginnifer Baxter stood up. "I'd be happy to —"

"Me too!" another girl interrupted.

Now they were all gathered around. I'd always wondered how to get girls' attention. All I had to do was mention Luke, I realized.

"If he wants graphics for his presentation," Angie Bilandic blurted, "I've got great sports photos. I could, uh, drop them off at his place."

"What's wrong with e-mail?" Jade Traxler sounded annoyed.

"Anything to save school sports," said Katelyn Ogleby, a cheerleader. "Luke could put photos to music. I've got a kickin' reggae version of the school fight song."

Seeing their eager faces gave me new hope. How could Luke tank with every girl at school dying to help him succeed?

"Du-u-u-u-u-u-u-u-u-u-u-u-ude!"

"Bulls pulled it out last night."

"Who stole my comb?"

I stood in the locker room after school, waiting for Luke. He hadn't returned my last three calls, so I went looking for him. The room was packed with jocks changing clothes, slamming lockers, and arguing about whether the Bulls would get pounded by the Celtics.

"Get lost, Polshek," a blond guy said. "Bulls are toast."

SNAP!

Polshek whipped a towel at the barrel-chested blond guy. Suddenly, the room turned into a battleground of snapping towels. I jumped out of the way. Where was Luke?

"Danny!?" I turned around, and there was Luke, pulling a T-shirt over his head. "What are you doing here?"

Towel-snapping came to a halt, and the guys looked up at me.

"Could we go somewhere, uh, private?" I asked Luke.

Luke motioned for me to follow. "Over here," he said, pointing to an empty bench.

"Where have you been?" I asked. Then I took a deep breath. "Everyone's counting on your speech. This is a big deal, Luke. You can't just be good — you've got to hit it out of the park."

"I'm not doing it."

My jaw dropped. "WHAT?"

"Not. Doing. It."

"But . . . !" I'd had a whole "You need to focus" pitch prepared. "Wh-what do you mean?"

He kicked the bench. "The speech reeks."

"No," I said. "No, no, no, no. You can't blow this off, Luke. We're in this together! I'll get blamed! People are counting on you to change the principal's mind!"

"Sorry." He looked at the floor.

"Listen, Luke," I begged. "I've got tons of ideas. We can make it into a show, with cool PowerPoint graphs and photos. Every girl in school is dying to help."

Luke looked suspicious. "How do you know?"

"I was at a Fashion Club meeting —" I started, but hesitated when Luke gave me a weird look. "Long story."

Luke sank onto the bench and put his head in his hands.

"You don't understand," he said. His face was sweating. "Kulbarsh gives me the creeps. I can't stand up there in front of him and everyone else."

Dr. Kulbarsh was intimidating. His bald head and unsmiling face made him look like an executioner.

He disapproved of everything — baggy pants, cell phones, kids in general. He rarely spoke except to say things like, "'Humongous' is not a real word."

"It's okay," I said, trying to reassure both of us. "You've just got a little stage fright. We'll fix that."

"No, we won't!" Luke said fiercely. "Every time I think about giving a speech in public, I want to barf. We're not going to fix that!" He stared at the floor.

I didn't know what to say. The coolest graphics in the world wouldn't help if Luke couldn't speak in public. The whole thing was going down in flames. Then I remembered something Ralph once told me. Maybe — maybe! — Luke would go for it.

"I think I have a cure for you," I said quietly.

Luke's eyes narrowed. "You do?"

"Yup," I said, with fake confidence. I had to work fast. I sat down and pulled out my notebook. I sketched furiously for a minute or so, then handed him a drawing.

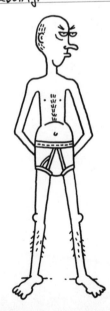

Luke picked it up and burst out laughing. "what the —?"

"You know Ralph, the janitor?" I said. "Well, he's an actor too. whenever he's nervous onstage? He pictures the audience in their underwear."

"That's good," admitted Luke.

"Kulbarsh is human," I said. "He burps and farts like everyone else."

"Draw him farting," Luke commanded.

I flipped to a new page in my sketchbook and started drawing again. Luke's eyes followed my hand.

"How do you do that?" he said.

"I don't know." I shrugged. "How do you hit a fastball?"

He shrugged too. A couple of jocks passed by, and Luke and I were silent until they were gone.

"Besides," I said. I was scared to bring up the subject again, but... "If you don't do the speech, Wagman'll flunk you."

Luke shrugged. "Yeah, so? School isn't my thing. I never remember facts, like who invented cars or where Portugal is. My brain's too crowded."

I tried to imagine.

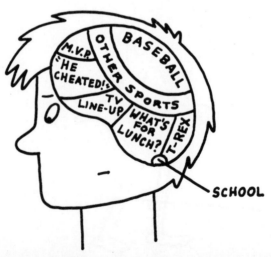

"In fact, I'd HATE school," Luke went on, "if it wasn't for sports. Baseball gives me a way to stand out. If I didn't have that ..." Luke shook his head. "I'd feel like a loser."

"A loser?" I couldn't believe it.

"Sometimes, baseball's the only thing that keeps me going," Luke said darkly.

This was good stuff, I realized. "That's what you should put in your speech, Luke." My voice rose. "Make it personal!"

Luke's face brightened for a half second... then clouded over again. "I don't know."

An eighth-grade soccer player passed by and saw Luke. "Hey, man. Good luck with that speech. If anyone can convince 'im, you can."

I didn't look at Luke, but waited for the comment to sink in. We both sat there a minute, until finally Luke picked a sock and some gym

shorts off the bench. It took me a second to
realize he was clearing a workspace.

"Crud." He sighed. "I can't fight everyone.
I'll try to do the stupid speech. But I'm not
promising anything."

YES!

Suddenly, my head felt a thousand times
lighter. Another crisis averted — kind of. But
keeping Luke on track wasn't going to be easy; I
was running through my bag of tricks. He shoved
aside some dirty towels, and we got started.

* CHAPTER TWELVE *

In the auditorium, a sea of parents, teachers, and students stared down at Pinky Shroeder. Behind the giant podium, Pinky looked even shorter than he was. You could tell he was overwhelmed.

"And that's why violent video games should be banned." Pinky's voice shook. "Except for Ninja Gangsta Bloodbath III and Overturned Tractor Trailer. They're okay. Oh, and Alien Attack Zone. And Executioner's Blade."

Pinky mopped his face with a tissue, as the principal sat stone-faced in his chair onstage. As usual, his face was totally unreadable.

* THE MANY MOODS OF PRINCIPAL KULBARSH

HAPPY

DISAPPROVING

EXCITED

FURIOUS

RELAXED

BALD

"Thank you, Pinky," said Mrs. Wagman, guiding him offstage. She took the mic and looked at her clipboard. "Next up — Luke Strohmer."

A few cheers, whistles, and woo-woos as Luke got up from his seat.

My stomach rumbled as I watched Luke walk down the aisle. He had a smile on his face, but I could see his clenched jaw and sweating forehead. There was a loud thump and a buzzing noise as he adjusted the mic. He looked at the crowd. "Um, hey, guys," he said.

In the hand that wasn't holding his speech, he picked up the clicker to control his PowerPoint presentation. He pressed a button, and the projection screen behind him showed a giant photo of the baseball team hugging and celebrating.

People cheered. Kulbarsh studied the ceiling.

Luke waited for the noise to die down and then cleared his throat. "Why Gerald Ford —"

He stopped. There was a long pause.

C'mon, Luke, I thought. You can do it.

"'Why Gerald Ford Needs After-School Sports,'" he said quietly.

"Speak into the mic!" called Jasper. Luke peered into the gloom, then started over.

"Sports and Gerald Ford go together like a hot dog and —" Luke stopped again, looking panicked.

"Mustard!" someone shouted, and people giggled.

Luke looked up, surprised. He clutched his piece of paper. "We need sports for a lot of reasons — not just 'cause the uniforms look cool." A few people laughed, and he stood up straighter. "Sports make us better students and," he mumbled, "better people."

Yeah, I thought. Keep going!

"I found out —" Luke looked up to the ceiling and sighed. Then he seemed to decide something. He looked out at the audience. "I found out a lot when I was working on this speech," he said. "Like how studies show that sports improve your

concentration. It actually makes you a better student. I'm serious." He clicked through some charts and graphs.

"Sports also improve self-esteem. There's a lot of research," Luke said, clicking to another chart. "Plus, I can vouch for it myself. I was never the world's best student." Luke gave a guilty shrug. "But baseball makes me look forward to school. Getting a hit makes me feel like I'm good at something. It's huge."

Luke's words were flowing more easily now.

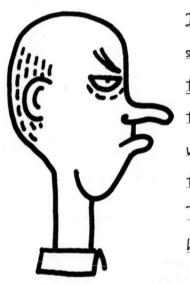

I was glad he'd made his speech more personal. Maybe this'll be okay after all, I thought. The crowd seemed with him, but it was hard to tell Luke's effect on Kulbarsh. The principal just stared, his mouth an unbroken line.

"Being on a team is a crazy amount of work." Luke clicked to a photo of the soccer team. "But it's worth it. The guys are like your brothers. You go through things together." He shook his head. "Like this spring, when we lost All-City."

The audience got very quiet.

My head snapped up; now Luke was really going off-script. He even put down his piece of paper. "After — you know — what happened," he went on, "I felt awful. Like I'd dragged the team down. To get our hopes up and then blow the game ... it just about killed me.

"It was like" — Luke's voice broke — "seeing joy slip out of your hands."

Even though I hated being reminded of the Incident, I could hear the truth in Luke's voice.

"But ..." Luke blinked. "I lived through it, right? I'm sure it was some kind of great learning experience or whatever."

Kulbarsh just stared.

"Anyway." Sounding more confident, Luke picked up his speech again. "Here's a graph that shows how sports improve your —" He clicked again.

Everyone gasped. I looked up and saw the screen.

My drawing.

HOLY CRUD!

"Oh, man!" Luke said. He clicked furiously, but the image didn't budge.

I looked back at Kulbarsh. The

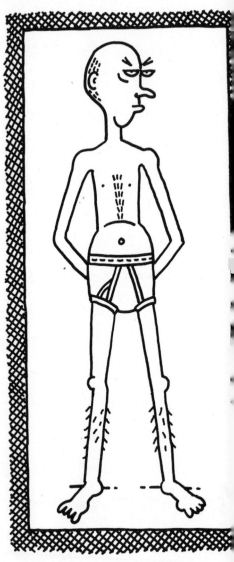

tips of his ears were beet red, and his nostrils were twitching furiously.

Nobody moved a muscle. The auditorium was silent.

Luke frantically clicked again. Nothing happened. NOOOOOOO! My drawing of the undressed principal was still up there on the screen, ten feet wide.

"HA HA HA HA HA HA HA HA HA HA!"

The audience exploded with laughter, like water bursting through a dam. People clutched their stomachs, rocked back and forth, pointed, gasped, sputtered, and howled.

I felt deeply sick to my stomach. How had those drawings gotten into the PowerPoint show?

It was THE ULTIMATE JINX!

Crud! Crud! Crud!

Kulbarsh stood up. His face had finally shifted — but not in a good way. I could barely look at his narrowed eyes and red face. I'd never seen him so angry. I buried my face in my hands.

"Mr. Strohmer." The crowd hushed to hear Kulbarsh's reaction. "To say you are in deep trouble is an understatement."

Luke was so stunned, he stopped fumbling with the clicker.

Kulbarsh continued. "You have disgraced the entire student body. From now on, we will no longer allow students to address the principal. You have single-handedly..." He glanced back at the screen. "FOR GOD'S SAKE, WILL YOU TAKE DOWN THAT DISGUSTING DRAWING?"

"I can't," Luke's voice was strangled. "The computer — froze."

Jasper ran up to the stage to help Luke, clicking on the mouse.

Kulbarsh smoothed his tie, like he was trying to compose himself. "I hope you're pleased, Mr. Strohmer."

Luke opened his mouth, but no words came

out. <u>CRUD!</u> Now his computer wasn't the only thing stuck. I sat there, watching helplessly as he tried to choke words out.

"I...ngh...mhph...uh..."

A second later, I was running down the aisle. Faster and faster, I bolted up the steps, picturing how very dead I was going to be.

When I hit the stage, I was out of breath. Pushing Luke aside, I pulled the mic down and turned toward the principal.

"It's not Luke's fault. I drew the cartoon,"
I announced. "I'm sorry you all had to see that."

By this time, Jasper had rebooted the laptop.
Thank God, I thought. Then he clicked the mouse, and the whole auditorium gasped again.

The farting principal filled the screen.

"Good Lord," Kulbarsh burst out.

* CHAPTER THIRTEEN *

Dr. Kulbarsh glared at me. Luke's mouth was open. Jasper's eyes widened. The audience was amazed. I was mortified.

"Excuse me?" Kulbarsh said in an exaggerated way.

"I'm Danny Shine," I said, nudging Luke farther out of the way. "I was the one who drew the cartoon. Cartoons," I corrected myself.

"I see." Kulbarsh waited.

Jasper clicked again and again, finally getting the "farting" pic off the screen. Kulbarsh stared like he was trying to melt me with his eyes.

"I'm sorry." My words felt hollow. "Really sorry. I just wanted to explain why . . . I made those drawings and gave them to Luke."

Luke gave me a puzzled look.

Kulbarsh sat down in his chair and leaned back with an evil chuckle. "This I'd like to hear."

I'd jumped onstage to take attention off Luke. But now that I had done it, I was

stumped. Looking down into the audience, I saw a disbelieving Phil Petrokis, a skeptical Velvet, and a thrilled Chantal.

What could I possibly say to save Luke and salvage his speech?

"Luke showed that cartoon, because..." Think of something — anything! "Because, um..." I bit my lip. "Because...because...sports teach you discipline. And how to deal with losing. And that's just as important as the Lincoln-Douglas debates and rational numbers and topic sentences.

"It's what makes some kids feel good about themselves," I continued. "For me, it's drawing hairy eyeballs. But everybody's got to have something. And sports are it for a lot of kids — what they work hard at and feel proud of. 'Cause without that pride or whatever? We'd all feel undressed."

There was some applause, but then Kulbarsh interrupted.

"Wait a minute." Kulbarsh frowned. "Where have I seen you before? Aren't you the one who blocked Luke's catch at the championships? The one who lost the game?"

Great, I thought. Now Kulbarsh will REALLY hate me.

"Yeah." I looked at the floor.

"I see." Kulbarsh lifted his chin, and his eyes got even narrower.

I should just leave now, I thought.

"And yet," Kulbarsh said slowly, "you're in favor of MORE sports funding?"

"I hate sports," I blurted out. "Climbing the rope in gym is torture. I don't know what a point spread is. And I hated them even more after, uh, what happened. When people got so mad about the game," I babbled, "it really freaked me out. But it also kind of — impressed me, in a weird way. Because they cared so much about their team. I don't know if I care that much about anything, except drawing and Rat Girl comics."

Some people smiled.

"So I hope you won't cut back after-school sports," I said to Kulbarsh. Now I was on a roll. "Because people feel REALLY strongly about this stuff — players _and_ fans. Maybe _too_ strongly. But at least they're excited about something, and there's way too little of that in life."

I paused.

"And if a sports-hating comics geek like _me_ feels that way..." I said. "Think how everyone else feels."

A few people started to applaud, and soon

everybody was clapping. Kulbarsh stood up and lifted his chin.

He cleared his throat.

"I'm not happy about that drawing," Kulbarsh said. "But I am ... intrigued to hear a defense of sports from YOU, a complete nonathlete. Someone who has never, in his entire time at Gerald Ford, had anything to do with sports. Or physical activity."

I felt my face get hot. Even though I'd said I hated sports, I didn't like being described as Mr. Anti-Jock.

"If someone like _you_ is fighting for the sports program," Kulbarsh said slowly, "maybe it _is_ worth keeping."

A hush spread over the audience. Then they stood up and roared.

Hey! I nudged Luke.

"It's just lucky for the school you got to speak," said Kulbarsh. "Right place, right time."

For once, I thought.

"Woo-hoo!" Chantal yelled. "Danny pulled it out! He saved school sports! Highland, watch out! 'Cause next year we're going to kick —"

"Enough, Chantal." Kulbarsh held up his hand.

"— YOUR BONY FREAKIN' BUTTS!!"

Everyone cheered again.

After assembly, a bunch of people came up to me onstage. But I grabbed Luke and pulled him over.

"WHAT HAPPENED WITH THE SLIDES?" I hissed. "When the underwear pic came on —"

"Oh, man." Luke buried his face in his hands. "I almost peed in my pants! I was using them while I practiced, like you said. Then I gave all my charts and graphs to my brother, so he could turn them into PowerPoint slides. I must have given him the cartoons too, by mistake."

I slapped my forehead. Why hadn't I made him do a practice run-through this morning?

"But you . . ." Luke's voice was quiet. "You didn't just save me — you saved sports. Now we'll have baseball next year. And I'll get another shot."

I looked up and saw we were surrounded. Luke's jock friends — Tank, Abs, and Kyle — were next to us, listening. I wondered if Luke would shrink back from his words, now that his friends were here.

"Hey, Jinx." Tank pointed at me. "I didn't know you could —"

"HE'S NOT A JINX!" Luke grabbed Tank's shirt.

"Whoa, whoa." Tank wriggled away. "All I said was —"

"Don't say it," Luke growled.

"But —" started Abs.

"He still lost the game for us," Chantal interrupted. She had edged her way to the front and planted herself in front of Luke. "That didn't change."

Luke gritted his teeth. "No, you're wrong." By now, the mob included Jasper, Axl, and even a curious teacher or two.

"Danny didn't lose the game for us." Luke's voice was fierce. "He did what everybody tries to do — catch a foul ball in the bleachers. Games are decided by what happens on the playing field, not in the stands. We're the ones who gave up those runs. Not Danny."

"But —" "No way —" "Nuh-uh —" people protested.

Luke held up his hand.

"WE lost the game. And we better face it. Otherwise we're not going to win any championship — ever. Blaming the Curse of the Woodchuck or the umpire or Danny is just messed up."

People looked at the floor, avoiding my eyes. Mrs. Wagman appeared at the edge of the crowd.

"Luke," she said. "Can I talk to you?"

Luke looked at the floor too.

"Are you going to flunk me?" he asked. "'Cause I still haven't finished giving a speech?"

"Well," said Wagman, "that's true, and I have to subtract points for that. But I happened to hear your defense of Danny just now. And that's the speech I'm basing your grade on."

"Huh?" Luke and I looked at each other.

"You expressed yourself perfectly," said Wagman. "You spoke out and took responsibility for what happened at the game. You backed up your argument persuasively. I'm giving you a B-plus."

Woo-hoo! Luke and I high-fived.

A few minutes later, Jasper found me in the crowd and gave me a fake karate chop.

"Well, the good news is everyone likes you again," said Jasper. "Or at least they don't dislike you. The bad news is, we still have school sports."

"Thanks." I laughed. "Where's Velvet?"

Jasper shrugged. "She could be anywhere," he said. "Clothes Town. Barrette Barn. The Chic Shack."

Something was different, obviously. "What happened?"

"She was always trying to change me," said Jasper. "'Comb your hair!' 'Don't wear a phone on your belt!' 'Take your cape off!'"

"And you felt insulted?"

"No." Jasper shook his head. "As a scientific experiment, I respected it. But she went too far."

"What'd she do?" I tried not to sound too eager.

"We were at my house, and I was showing her some collectible action figures," Jasper said.

"Droids, orcs, Rat Girl in the original packaging," he continued. "'You should get rid of these dolls,' she said. She actually used that word."

"Oh, no." I winced.

"Dolls!" he repeated, shaking his head.

"Geez."

"That's when I realized how huge the gap between us really was," he said.

"Yeah." I nodded. "Hey. Want to watch Attack of the Mutant Gym Teachers tonight?"

"YES!"

"WAIT UP!" Tank yelled from down the hall. Assuming he was talking to someone else, I kept walking. But then he tapped me on the arm. "Hey, Danny."

I turned around and saw Abs, Kyle, and Tank. Had he ever used my actual name before?

I felt a wave of resentment. Apparently, now that Luke had given his little speech, I was no longer radioactive. "Let me guess," I said sarcastically. "You forgive me?"

Tank looked sheepish. "Uh, no." He swallowed. "We came to ask if YOU can forgive US."

Me... forgive them?

"'Cause I know we were kind of unfair to you," he admitted.

I didn't know what to say. "Um..."

"Those cartoons today were good," said Kyle. "I like how you draw farts."

"Uh, thanks." Had anyone ever said that to Picasso?

"We were wondering..." Tank suddenly seemed shy. "At games, we're tired of the same old face paint. I bet you could do something pretty cool."

Me? Painting faces of lunatic fans? Was he crazy?

"I guess so," I said.

"Sweet." Tank and Abs high-fived. "Could you paint, like, a really scary, insane, rude Woody Woodchuck?"

"Um..." I tried to imagine it.

"We could pay you, even. Free tix to games. Team jerseys. Golf balls."

"That's, uh, tempting." Not!

But I knew I'd probably do it anyway.

"So." Abs played with his zipper. "You could forgive us?"

I realized I already had.

"Okay," I said. "Yeah."

"YES!" They bumped knuckles and started rattling off other violent face-painting ideas. "Poison cobra! Bloody knife! Oozing —"

Someone ran by and nearly knocked me over. I spun around — it was Asia! My stomach did its usual flip-flop. Thinking about her hearing my wimpy-guy plea to Kulbarsh was embarrassing.

"Hey, Danny." She patted my back. "Way to surprise everyone! Great job! I just have one question."

I nodded.

"If you hate sports so much..." She lowered her voice. "Why'd you agree to go to the game when I asked?"

I looked at her carefully. Her lips were pressed into a tiny smile, but it was impossible to tell what she was thinking. Did she know why I'd said yes that day?

"Uhhhh..." I stammered.

"Oops, gotta run," she said, looking at her watch. "I'm late for African drumming!"

"But —" It seemed like we always got interrupted.

She gave me a big wave and took off. As she whipped around a corner, something flew out of her messenger bag. I walked over to see what she'd dropped.

Her favorite comic. What a stroke of luck!
Now I had the perfect excuse to stop by her
locker tomorrow.

Slipping it into my backpack, I smiled.

Finally, I was unjinxed.

<u>H.N. KOWITT</u> has written more than forty books for younger readers, including The Loser List series, <u>Dracula's Decomposition Book</u>, <u>This Book Is a Joke</u>, and <u>The Sweetheart Deal</u>. She lives in New York City, where she enjoys cycling, flea markets, and gardening on her fire escape. You can find her online at www.kowittbooks.com.

Danny Shine just wants to draw comics, buy comics, and talk about comics. But first, he has to get his name off of

Read them all!

When the new guy threatens Danny's
comic-drawing dreams, it's time for